JUMPING INTO NOTHING

JUMPING INTO NOTHING

by **Gina Willner-Pardo**

Illustrated by **Heidi Chang**

CLARION BOOKS ○ New York

Clarion Books
a Houghton Mifflin Company imprint
215 Park Avenue South, New York, NY 10003
Text copyright © 1999 by Gina Willner-Pardo
Illustrations copyright © 1999 by Heidi Chang

Type is 15-point Adobe Caslon.
Illustrations executed in pencil.

Printed in the USA.

Library of Congress Cataloging-in-Publication Data
Willner-Pardo, Gina.
Jumping into nothing / by Gina Willner-Pardo ; illustrated by Heidi Chang.
p.   cm.
Summary: Nine-year-old Sophie tries to deal with her fear of jumping off the
high diving board at the community pool by listing other things she is afraid of
doing and forcing herself to do them.
ISBN 0-395-84130-5
[1. Fear—Fiction. 2. Swimming pools—Fiction.] I. Chang, Heidi, ill. II. Title.
PZ7.W683675Ju   1999
[Fic]—dc21   98-26144
CIP
AC

KPT 10 9 8 7 6 5 4 3 2 1

For Tracy, who helps me find courage.
—G. W.-P.

For C.T., who always gets it.
—H.C.

CHAPTER 1

It was only June, a Tuesday, the first week of summer vacation. You could tell that summer was new because all the kids at the Bancroft Hills Community Pool were doing cannonballs off the diving board and screaming their heads off. Tina the lifeguard was blowing her whistle and yelling for the boys to quit pushing. The moms looked red and blotchy and embarrassed for everyone to be seeing their legs.

By August the kids would be practicing

back dives and half twists. Tina would be too busy flirting with the swim team coach to notice any pushing. The moms would have had time to work on their tans and get used to walking around without jeans and baggy sweaters. Pretty much everyone would have stopped screaming.

I loved summer. Some kids had to move or go visit their dads' new families in New Jersey. My best friend, Annalise, took Drama in summer school. I got to sleep in and stay up late. In between I took Math Discoveries and hung out at the Bancroft Hills Community Pool. Usually the pool is the best thing about summer. The only things you have to worry about are Mario Esposito giving you a wedgie and the vending machine running out of grape soda.

Usually.

That Tuesday, I had just finished my lunch, except for half a ham sandwich and a spoonful of macaroni salad. I lay on my pink

and green beach towel waiting for Annalise and listening to my stomach digest my food. The sun shone red through my closed eyelids. I saw little black dots floating around and wondered if they were atoms.

"Hey!" I heard Annalise say.

I opened my eyes.

"How was Drama?" I asked.

Annalise plunked down on her backpack and bent over to unbuckle her sandals.

"Lousy," she said. "I had to be a spoon."

I laughed. *Beauty and the Beast* had only a couple of good parts for girls. Everyone wanted to be Belle or Mrs. Potts.

"If you can't sing, they make you be silverware," Annalise said. She stood up, unzipped her backpack, and pulled out a striped towel. "At least I wasn't a fork."

I wasn't sure why being a spoon was better than being a fork, but I nodded so Annalise would know I was glad for her.

Annalise arranged her towel next to mine.

"Let's get really hot," she said, stretching out on her stomach.

Annalise liked getting really hot before she got into the pool. That way, she said, you appreciated how nice it was to be cool and wet. Also, you didn't stand on the stairs shivering and looking stupid, the way some of the moms did.

I was already pretty hot, but I said "OK." Going in with Annalise was more fun than going in by myself. We liked making faces underwater and seeing who could swim the farthest without taking a breath.

We lay there for a while. I could feel sweat drops running down my neck. I wished I had a little bit of grape soda left to drink.

Suddenly there was shade. I opened my eyes. Maggie Dobleman and Jennifer Mayberry were standing over us, tall and thin and drippy with pool water.

Maggie and Jennifer were the coolest girls in our class. Maggie wore diamond stud earrings. Once she dyed part of her hair blue and said her mother didn't mind. Jennifer wore a retainer with glittery gold stars all over it. She could sing the Flintstones song underwater. She was always talking about her parents' summer house in the country.

Both Maggie and Jennifer were very tan. I wondered how they'd had time to get so tan since last Thursday, when school let out.

I was glad for the shade. But Maggie and

Jennifer could be mean. The sweat cooled on my skin. I shivered a little.

"You guys want to do something?" Maggie asked. The way she talked made you think that maybe she wasn't talking to you at all. Or that if she was, she didn't care whether you heard her or not.

"Like what?" Annalise asked.

"Race," Jennifer said. "Jump off the high dive."

"Oh," Annalise said. "Let's do that."

I shot Annalise a look. A look that I hoped said, *Are you crazy?*

"I love the high dive," Annalise said.

She hadn't even seen my look. She had forgotten about me and the high dive. How I hated it. How I had to back down the ladder every time. How I always said, "I'm never trying to jump off the high dive ever again. Ever."

Ever.

Annalise was standing up. She pulled up the straps of her suit.

"Come on, Sophie," she said. "It'll be fun."

"Chicken!" Maggie said. "Sophie's chicken!" She wrapped her towel around her like a cloak.

I hoisted myself out of the pool.

"Shut up, Maggie," I said. I thought about reminding her how last year she had to be in the slow reading group. But it was summer now. Nobody remembered about the slow reading group in summer.

Also, I'm not the kind of kid who reminds other kids about what's wrong with them.

"At my pool in the country the high dive is much higher than this," Jennifer said. "At my pool in the country everybody can jump off the high dive."

"It's scary," Annalise said. "I remember how it felt before I did it the first time." She stopped to suck on her wet braid. "Like jumping into nothing," she said.

I knew she was trying to be nice. She was letting me know she understood how I felt.

I thought how Annalise and I both liked milk chocolate honeycomb and getting phone calls and reading about outer space. We were both going to be veterinarians and we were both 85 percent sure that we weren't going to get married.

We both liked everything the same. The way best friends always did.

Maggie put one arm around Jennifer's

shoulders and one arm around Annalise's. Annalise looked smiley-proud and embarrassed all at once.

"*We* like the high dive," Maggie announced, "and Sophie's chicken!"

I wanted to tell her to shut up again, but I didn't. I felt too miserable. I *was* chicken.

And Annalise looked like she was having an awful lot of fun being part of "we."

○

"The thing is," Annalise said, "just to do it."

"It's too high," I said. "Too scary."

We were sitting outside the pool's front gate, waiting for Annalise's mom to pick us up. Kids were pouring out into the parking lot, laughing, smelling like chlorine and sunscreen. A lot of the boys were swatting each other with towels. Nobody looked scared.

"How do you just do something scary?" I

asked. "Without crying or wetting your pants or throwing up?"

"I was scared to go to kindergarten," Annalise said. "I threw up the first day. Then I kicked Mrs. Hightower in the shins."

"Really?"

Annalise nodded.

"My mom stayed with me for the whole first day," she said. "Until I got used to it. Then half the second day. By the end of the first week I could go alone."

I sighed.

"I don't think my dad is going to stand on the high dive with me until I get used to it," I said.

"I guess not," Annalise said.

But Annalise had given me an idea.

"Maybe I just need to practice," I said. "Maybe I just need to do something a little scarier every day. Maybe by the time I get up to jumping off the high dive, it won't seem so scary."

"Maybe," Annalise said.

It was worth a try, I decided.

Still, the best thing about my plan was that I didn't have to jump off the high dive any time soon.

Annalise sighed.

"Wasn't it cool?" she said.

"What?"

"The way they just came up to us," Annalise said. "The way they just asked us if we wanted to hang out with them. I think they're really starting to like us."

"Like *you*, you mean," I said. "They called me chicken."

"Maybe next year they'll want to eat lunch with us. Maybe they'll save seats for us at assemblies. Maybe we can all do a Science Fair project together."

I didn't say anything. Best friends were supposed to want the same things. I didn't feel like telling Annalise that I wanted Maggie and Jennifer to get hit by a bus.

Annalise grabbed my arm.

"You *have* to figure out a way to jump off that high dive," she said. "Our whole future depends on it."

When Annalise said it like that, it sounded serious. Like maybe she wouldn't want to be best friends with a chicken.

Even a chicken who understood about being a spoon.

CHAPTER 2

The next day Annalise hurried across the pavement around the edge of the pool. She was barefoot. I could tell the pavement was hot because Annalise hopped from puddle to puddle.

"Did you think of any scary things?" she asked after she'd made it to our spot on the grass.

"Five," I said, pulling my list from the pocket of my backpack.

"Let's see," she said.

This is what I had written down.

```
┌─────────────────────────────────────┐
│  Scary Things to do:                 │
│  ─────────────────────────────       │
│  1. Do a math problem on             │
│     the board.                       │
│  2. Sleep without my                 │
│     night-light.                     │
│  3. Tell Matthew Latiano             │
│     I think he's cute.               │
│  4. Eat some bugs.                   │
│  5. Ride my bike without             │
│     holding the handlebars.          │
└─────────────────────────────────────┘
```

"What kind of bugs?" Annalise asked.

"Ants or grasshoppers," I said. "Maybe a worm, if I can get up my nerve."

"Wow," Annalise said. "That would be really brave. Brave and gross at the same time."

She paused. "Do you think that after doing all those things, you'll feel any braver about jumping off the high dive?" she asked.

"I don't know," I said. "But maybe it's like your mother staying with you on the first day of kindergarten. Maybe after doing a lot of scary things, jumping into nothing won't seem so scary."

We sat in silence for a while. I offered Annalise one of my pickles. She held it delicately between two fingers, as if it were a slug.

"Do you really think Matthew Latiano is cute?" she asked.

"Kind of," I admitted.

Annalise's eyes got big.

"Wow," she said.

○

I hate math. At regular school I am always forgetting 7 × 9 and the right way to read a graph, which is why I always have to take Math Discoveries in the summer. My mother is an engineer and she says that everyone has to know about math. Even nurses and police officers. Even people with computers.

The main thing I hate about math is that it's never over. Just when you get the hang of addition, you have to learn subtraction. There's always something else.

The other thing I hate about math is that a lot of times you have to do it on the board. It's not like spelling, which only the teacher sees, or reading, which is private.

But Dad always says there's no time like the present. So I decided to volunteer to do math on the blackboard right away.

"Let's do some problems on the board," Mrs. Watson said at eleven fifteen. "Five volunteers for five problems."

My throat closed up. My hands started to sweat. My stomach felt as though it had jumped into my chest.

Slowly I raised my hand.

"Sophie! Good!" Mrs. Watson said. She held out a piece of chalk and I stood up to take it from her.

"Why don't you try problem number one?" she said. I copied the problem from the book onto the board:

$$9 \times 5 =$$

I was shaking so hard that my nine came out looking like a seven. I had to erase and start over.

It was awful, standing there thinking. All the other kids went faster than I did. Mary-Claire Mitchell finished problem number four in about twenty-three seconds and went back to her desk. I kept thinking, *What if there's a big piece of toilet paper hanging down my leg?*

It was just awful.

"Let's look at number one," Mrs. Watson said after I'd sat down. "Any trouble here?"

I held my breath. I was pretty sure that 9×5 equaled 45, even though my heart was hammering so hard that I almost couldn't hear myself think.

"OK," Mrs. Watson said. "How about number two?"

And that was all. Nothing. Nobody laughed. Nobody whispered. I didn't have toilet paper hanging down my leg. I hadn't forgotten to tuck in my shirt.

And 9×5 *did* equal 45.

○

"How did it feel?" Annalise wanted to know at the pool that afternoon.

"OK," I said. "Like maybe I could do another math problem at the board someday."

"How about jumping off the high dive?" Annalise asked.

"No," I said. "Not yet."

Annalise looked disappointed.

"Don't rush me," I said.

We headed toward the vending machine for grape sodas. Too late, I saw Maggie and Jennifer signing in at the front desk.

Maggie saw Annalise and smiled.

"Want to jump off the high dive?" she asked.

She didn't even look at me.

"Sure," Annalise said. "In a minute."

Jennifer hooked a lock of hair back behind her ear.

"Hurry," she said. "We need three to play Pirates Walking the Plank."

Annalise waited until they were far enough away.

"They don't need three to play Pirates," she said. "They could play with four. Jennifer's just being mean."

"They *are* mean," I said. "What do you want to play with them for, anyway?"

"I don't know," Annalise said. "I don't *really* want to play with them." She seemed to be thinking. "I just like that they want to play with us."

She stuttered a little when she said "us." I knew she'd almost said "me."

"I'll only play a little while," Annalise said. I nodded.

"Anyway, I *like* jumping off the high dive," Annalise said. She sounded almost angry. "You'd like it, too. If you'd just do it."

Annalise played with Maggie and Jennifer until Jennifer's mom picked them up. Jennifer had an appointment with the orthodontist. I knew from my babysitter that all you did at Dr. Biemer's was sit in a big chair while he looked in your mouth and tightened up your retainer. Jennifer made it sound like she was going to Disneyland.

At first, while they were jumping off the high dive, I pretended to be asleep. But after a while, I let myself watch. Annalise marched fearlessly along the length of the board. She stood at the very end, her toes curled over the tip, her arms down at her sides. She looked straight ahead. I wondered what she could see up there that I was missing.

Then she jumped. She kept herself straight and skinny, like a pencil. In no time at all she was in the water. It took maybe two seconds.

You'd think nothing that lasted two seconds could be so bad.

Annalise came back to our towels after Maggie and Jennifer left for the day. I could tell that she felt funny. As if she had left me out of something really fun.

"I love to watch you jump off the high dive," I said.

Annalise looked relieved that I wasn't mad.

"Really?"

I nodded.

"You stand so straight," I said. "You make hardly any splash."

I was already miserable. There was no reason for Annalise to be miserable too.

Annalise smiled. She glanced over at the old tetherball pole.

"Look," she said.

I could see Matthew Latiano and Mario Esposito sitting in the dust.

There's no time like the present.

"Wait here," I told Annalise.

I walked over to the tetherball pole. For the second time that day, my hands got sweaty and my stomach flopped around. Doing scary things really gave you a workout.

Matthew and Mario were seeing how hard they could bite their arms without bleeding.

"Hey, Mario," I said.

Mario took his arm out of his mouth. "Yeah?"

"Can I talk to Matthew for a minute?"

Mario nudged Matthew in the ribs and said "Oooh." Then he got up and ran back toward the pool.

"What?" Matthew asked, standing up.

I took a deep breath.

"Your're not . . . terrible," I said.

It was as close as I could get to telling him he was cute.

Boy, did I feel like an idiot.

Matthew was OK, though.

"You, either," he said.

We stood around for a minute. I couldn't think of anything else to say.

Finally Matthew pointed to one of the moms dangling her feet in the shallow end.

"Mrs. Avery's got the veiniest legs of any mom at the pool," he said.

"I was watching her once when she didn't know it. She was picking her teeth," I said proudly.

"Wow," Matthew said.

○

"He really is cute," I told Annalise later that afternoon.

"You're two for two," Annalise said. "Pretty soon you're going to be the bravest kid at the pool."

"Maybe," I said. My hands didn't sweat nearly as much when I told Matthew he wasn't terrible as when I volunteered to do problem number one.

Maybe I was getting braver after all.

CHAPTER 3

That night when Dad came in to say good night he said, "Hey! It's dark in here."

"Yeah," I said. My voice sounded whispery and little in the blackness.

Dad picked up the night-light sitting on my shelf.

"Did the bulb burn out?" he asked.

"No," I said. "I'm just ready to sleep in the dark now."

"You are?" Dad sat on the edge of the bed. I nodded.

"Dad?" I said. "What are you afraid of?"

Dad sighed.

"Things I don't even want to talk about."

"Like what?"

He was quiet. Then he said, "Flying artichokes."

"Dad!"

"Forgetting how to chew. Pigs with no clothes on."

Now I was laughing.

"Lots of things," Dad said.

When I stopped laughing, he said, "Why don't you tell me what scares you?"

I didn't want to tell him about the high dive. I knew what he'd say. That there was nothing wrong with being scared. That it wasn't a good idea to do something just because somebody made fun of you if you didn't.

"I don't know," I said. "Being afraid, maybe."

Dad nodded.

"That's the worst," he said.

I sighed.

Dad leaned down and kissed my forehead.

"I slept with a night-light until I was sixteen," he said. "Did I ever tell you that?"

"I can't remember."

"Well, it's true," he said. "Honest."

"I believe you," I said.

"Your mother is afraid when she gives lectures," Dad said.

Even though Dad and Mom are divorced, Dad always likes to mention her. I think he wants me to know he hasn't forgotten all about her.

"Once, before a speech, she had to put a paper bag over her head and take deep breaths," Dad said.

"I think you told me that once," I said.

"Everyone's afraid of something," he said.

Not Maggie Dobleman. Not Jennifer Mayberry.

Not Annalise.

"Night-light's here if you want it," Dad said.

Then he was gone.

Nighttime isn't really black. It's shadowy gray and fuzzy. You can almost see things.

It isn't quiet, either. You can hear water gurgling in the pipes in the wall. Cats fighting down the street. Wind.

Wind is the worst. Because then you have to remind yourself that there are no such things as ghosts and that if it was a burglar, Dad would hear and call the police.

Finally I fell asleep. Finally.

○

Wednesday morning I decided to ride my bike to math class.

"Wear your helmet!" Dad called from the front door.

I waited until I got to Vandenburg Boulevard. Vandenburg Boulevard has wide sidewalks without a lot of bumps and cracks.

I waited until I got going. I almost closed my eyes trying to picture how I would look, relaxed and steady and sure that I wouldn't fall.

Then I let go.

I think I stayed up for a couple of seconds. I think maybe I got so excited about not falling down that I forgot to concentrate. Or maybe there was a pebble I didn't see.

But suddenly there I was, all in a heap, tangled up in my own arms and legs. Which hurt.

If I'd been in my own backyard, I would have cried a lot. But I didn't feel like crying on Vandenburg Boulevard with cars whizzing by, full of dads and moms in suits.

So I stood up. I felt like I was collecting my arms and legs from all over the sidewalk. My ankle was bleeding and I'd skinned both my elbows.

I had to walk my bike to Math Discoveries. My ankle was killing me. I kept thinking, *What if I'd really hurt myself? Broken my leg, or cracked my head open?*

○

"At least I did it," I told Annalise at the pool. "I guess."

"So that's good," Annalise said.

"Maybe not," I said. "I mean, maybe sometimes you're supposed to be afraid. So you don't end up bleeding all over the sidewalk."

Or floating face down in the pool.

"How can you tell?" I asked. "When you're supposed to be afraid and when you're not?"

"I don't know," Annalise said.

We were out on the edge of the grass, far away from most of the other kids.

"Maybe this would be a good time to eat an ant or something," I said.

It seemed like a good idea to eat ants someplace where not a whole lot of people would see you.

We looked in the grass.

"How about a pill bug?" Annalise said.

"Too big," I said.

Finally we found ants crawling in and out of a crack in the pavement.

"Just looking at them makes my stomach wavy," Annalise said.

"I wish I could tell which ones are babies," I said. "I hate to think of eating a baby."

We were quiet, watching the ants.

"I think," Annalise said, "that maybe you can't think too much."

And then I just did it. Fast, so I wouldn't

have to think anymore. I smushed a couple of ants under my finger, brought my finger to my mouth, and licked the ants off.

"Gross!" Annalise whispered in horror.

"Blecch!" I said, swallowing. "Oh, blecch, blecch, blecch!"

I ran to the drinking fountain. I drank water until my stomach ached, until Tina

had to blow her whistle and yell for me to give the kids behind me a turn.

"I can still feel them!" I said to Annalise. "It's like they're still walking around inside me!"

"That's impossible," Annalise said.

"You don't think they're still alive, do you?" I asked. "You don't think they're going to live inside of me and build nests and lay eggs, do you?"

"No."

"You don't think they'll have to operate to get them out?"

"Absolutely not," Annalise said.

"I wish I'd done some research," I said. "Just so I'd know for sure."

We settled ourselves on our towels. Annalise said, "Now you've done everything. All five things."

"Yeah," I said. I did feel proud.

"It's still June," Annalise said. "If you jump off the high dive now, Maggie and Jennifer will forget all about you being chicken by September."

Maggie and Jennifer showed up around two. They draped their towels over some deck chairs and smeared sunscreen on their arms. I could tell they were sneaking looks at Matthew Latiano and Mario Esposito practicing their racing dives. Maggie and Jennifer were giggling and talking more loudly than usual, but Matthew and Mario didn't pay any attention to them.

I liked thinking that Matthew was the kind of boy who was more impressed by Mrs. Avery picking her teeth than by a shrieky girl with diamond earrings and blue hair. Thinking that made me feel brave.

Maggie and Jennifer got tired of trying to attract the boys' attention. They saw us and came over.

"Who wants to jump off the high dive?" Maggie asked.

I took a deep breath.

"Me," I said. "I do."

"You do?" Jennifer asked.

I nodded. I hated them so much, just then. The way they tried to get the boys to look at them. The way Maggie asked who wanted to jump off the high dive. As if she knew I would rather do anything else.

Annalise clapped me on the back.

"Cool," she said. Her smile was enormous.

○

Maggie went first. She walked out to the end of the board. From the ground, I could see her toes curling over the edge.

She jumped. In less than a second she was underwater.

Jennifer was next.

"Watch me!" she yelled, fixing her goggles just so. She jumped and held her arms out like wings. "I'm a giant housefly!" she yelled just before she splashed.

Annalise grabbed the handrails.

"Remember," she said, leaning backward,

"you ate ants. You can do anything you want."

She looked up the ladder and started to climb.

I stood at the base of the ladder and watched Annalise climb higher and higher and get smaller and smaller. Then, hoisting herself up off the ladder, she stood on the board for a minute. Another minute, and she was out of sight. A second later I heard her splash.

I began to climb. I climbed and climbed. The worst thing was everything looking smaller and smaller.

Two steps from the top of the ladder I stopped climbing.

"Come on, Sophie!" Annalise yelled. She had pulled herself out of the water and was standing by the edge of the pool next to Maggie and Jennifer, hugging herself to keep from shivering.

She looked the same size as a mushroom, a blade of grass, a drawing of a girl in a book. She looked small. She did not look real.

Slowly, I felt with my foot for the next lowest rung. I began to back down.

"I knew it," Maggie said loudly to Jennifer, arms folded in front of her in satisfaction. "I knew she was chicken."

In the movies, if you heard someone say that, you would stop backing down. You would bite your lip to keep from shaking. Somehow you would find courage. You would make your way to the top of the ladder and out along the board. And you would jump.

And in September Maggie and Jennifer would fight for the seat next to yours at assemblies.

That's what would have happened in the movies.

◎

Later, after Maggie and Jennifer had gone home, Annalise found me in the shallow end.

"What are you doing?" she asked.

"Floating," I said. "Letting myself float."

"Face down?"

"It's relaxing," I said. "I like the way everybody's legs look all wavy and blue. I like not being able to hear what anybody's saying."

Annalise examined one of her braids.

"It wasn't so bad," she said.

"It was terrible," I said. "Awful."

"Nobody even noticed. Except for Jennifer and Maggie and me," Annalise said. "Matthew and Mario were doing underwater handstands. They didn't see a thing."

"I think I'm just going to float some more," I said.

But it was nice to know about Matthew and Mario doing handstands.

"I've been thinking," Annalise said. "Maybe I'm getting kind of tired of the high dive."

I didn't say anything.

"I miss making faces underwater," Annalise said. "I mean, how many times can you jump off the high dive?"

"You won't be cool next year," I said.

"I wasn't cool last year," Annalise said. "I'm kind of used to it."

I smiled. I had missed Annalise. I was glad that she was sick of the high dive, and Maggie and Jennifer. It almost made everything all right.

Almost.

CHAPTER 4

The first week in August, Dad and I camped out in the backyard. We lay on top of our sleeping bags and ate Hershey's Kisses and tried to guess how many frogs were croaking. We watched the stars wink on. Dad tried to find Orion's belt, mainly because it is the only constellation he knows.

"It's brighter out here than in my room," I said.

"Your room is like a cave without that night-light," Dad said. "How can you stand to sleep in a room so dark?"

"I don't know," I said. "I just got used to it."

"My brave girl," Dad said.

For no reason, my eyes filled up with tears.

"Not brave at all," I said.

I wondered if Dad could hear that I was crying.

"I'm scared of everything," I said. "Being left out. Not being cool." I swallowed. "Jumping off the high dive."

Dad was quiet. Finally he said, "You *are* cool."

Even though I was irritated, I smiled up into the blackness. I knew he would say that.

"And I can help you with the high dive," Dad said.

○

For twenty-five dollars, the Bancroft Hills Community Pool gave you a key. The key unlocked the gates to the pool. You could swim whenever you wanted. Tina wasn't there, though, so you had to be careful. Dad

had a key. He went swimming every morning at six o'clock. "When it's quiet," he said.
"When you can hear yourself think."

I had never been to the pool so early in the
day. The life jackets and kickboards were all
stacked up by the lifeguard's chair. The only
sound was from the cars passing by. The
water was still, like an upside-down sky.

"Try it now," Dad said.

The high dive looked just as high as always.
Like a giant crane.

I shook my head.

"I don't know," I said.

Dad shrugged.

"It doesn't matter," he said.

But it did. To me.

"Maybe I'll just see what everything looks
like from up there," I said.

I climbed and climbed. This time I remembered about looking down. Instead, I made
myself look at my hands. I made myself look
up.

Finally I reached the top of the ladder. The

board stretched out ahead, its pebbly, hard-rubber whiteness like a giant tongue.

I pulled myself up onto it. My legs felt like straws trying to hold up a table.

But the view was interesting. The early-morning air was blue and cool. A light, wobbly

breeze blew across the pool, wrinkling the water.

"Hey! I can see Vandenburg Boulevard," I said.

The people, the cars and buses, the trees growing along the curb looked like plastic toys.

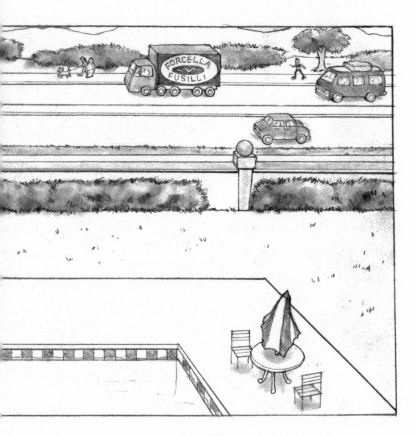

"Pretty, isn't it?" Dad called from the ground.

It was. I got a funny feeling in the back of my throat, looking down at the people and cars on Vandenburg Boulevard. Like the feeling I got sucking on a really strong peppermint. A feeling that the world was brand-new washed and clean.

"It's nice to be able to just look," I said. "Without being rushed."

My heart had stopped hammering.

"It's so pretty," I said.

I started to walk. I didn't let myself think about how high up I was, or how people who had fallen off of skyscrapers looked on TV.

I looked out into nothing.

And I jumped.

It was over so fast. It takes more time to sneeze than it took to fall.

When I hit the water, I could have come right up. But I stayed underwater for an extra second. Just to be alone with how good I felt.

Then I came up. Dad was smiling.

"I was going to say 'Take your time,'" he said. "But you didn't give me a chance."

That afternoon, Annalise and I jumped off the high dive for an hour. We jumped with our eyes closed. We tried to see how much of "The Star-Spangled Banner" we could sing before we hit the water. I got up to "dawn's."

We played Pirates Walking the Plank. With just two.

I knew Maggie and Jennifer saw us. They pretended not to. They spent a lot of time sitting on the jets in the Jacuzzi and watching bubbles blow up under their bathing suits.

"You can ask them to play, if you want," I said to Annalise as we made our way around to the ladder.

"Why would I want to do that?" Annalise asked. "It's more fun with just us."

○

Afterward we lay on our towels to get warm. I almost fell asleep watching drops of pool water evaporate off my arm.

"Your plan worked," Annalise whispered. "You got used to being scared."

"Not really," I said.

"Mrs. Potts has a much more interesting part than the spoons," Annalise said. "But she has to sing." She sighed. "I'm afraid to sing in front of other people."

"You have a nice voice," I said, to be a good friend.

Annalise shook her head.

"Not in front of other people." She looked at me. "Maybe I should make a list of things that scare me. Maybe I can get used to singing in public."

"I don't think it will work," I said.

"How come?"

I thought for a minute.

"I didn't get used to being scared," I said. "I was just as scared on the high dive today as I was at the beginning of the summer."

"Then how come you jumped?" Annalise asked.

"I don't know, exactly," I said. "I was just ready. I wasn't ready in June, but I was today."

Annalise scrunched up her face.

"You mean you ate ants for nothing?"

"I think so," I said. "I don't think you should practice being scared the way you

practice cartwheels. I think it's better if you just wait for the right time."

Annalise smiled.

"That's a relief," she said. "Petting a slug was going to be on my list."

"Sometimes my dad says there's no time like the present. And sometimes he says, 'What's your hurry?'" I said.

"They're always telling you things," Annalise said.

"I guess you just have to know when it's time to do something, and when it's time to wait. And when it's something you shouldn't do at all," I added, remembering about riding my bike with no hands.

"That's a lot to know," Annalise said.

"It's too bad you can't take it in summer school," I said.

But I was glad that you couldn't. Dad would probably have signed me up. And there were only three weeks of summer left.

Three weeks to play Pirates Walking the Plank. With just two.